Little
Spook

by Penny Dolan and Joshua Heinsz

W
FRANKLIN WATTS
LONDON•SYDNEY

Little Spook was at the window
with his sister, Susie Spook.
He looked at the moon in the sky.
It was getting dark.

"Oh no!" he said.

"I don't want to go out.

I'm scared."

3

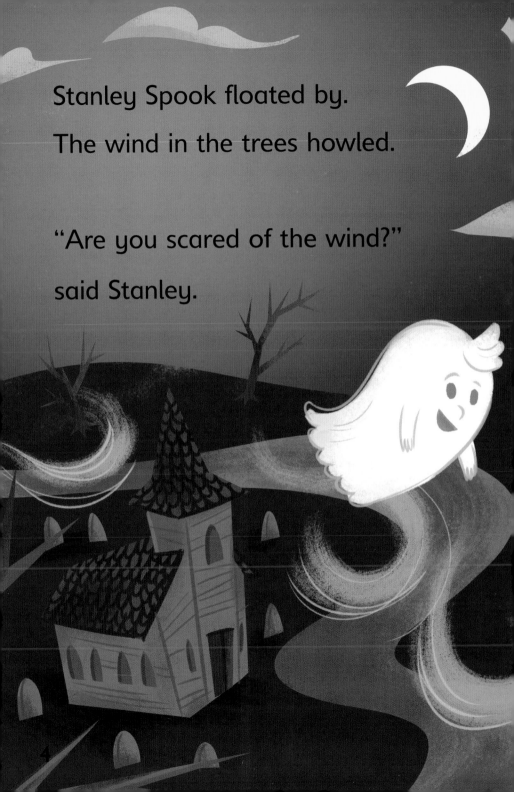

Stanley Spook floated by.

The wind in the trees howled.

"Are you scared of the wind?"

said Stanley.

4

Little Spook shook his head.

"No, not the wind," he said.

Then Uncle Spook floated by.
The owl in the tree hooted.

"Is it the owl that makes you
scared?" said Uncle Spook.

"No, it's not the owl,"

said Little Spook.

Then Aunty Spook floated by.
Her bats flapped all round her.

"Are you scared of my bats?"
she said.

"No, I'm not scared of them,"

said Little Spook.

Mum and Dad came in
to see what was going on.

"Is it my cats?" said Mum.

"Is it me? Am I too scary?"
said Dad.

"No," said Little Spook.

"Then what **are** you scared of?"
everyone said.

"I don't want to go out,"
said Little Spook.

"I'm scared of the dark!"

"Hello!" said a little voice.
Everyone looked down.
They saw a firefly.

"I can help you, Little Spook,"
said the firefly.
"I have a bright light in my tail."

Little Spook let the firefly
rest on his hand.
The firefly's light got brighter
and brighter.

Little Spook smiled.

"I am not scared now," he said.

"Thank you."

So Little Spook and the firefly
went out into the dark night,
and Little Spook was not scared
at all.

Story order

Look at these 5 pictures and captions.
Put the pictures in the right order
to retell the story.

1

A firefly came to the window.

2

Little Spook went outside.

3

The firefly lit up the dark.

4

Little Spook was scared of the dark.

5

Everyone tried to help.

Independent Reading

This series is designed to provide an opportunity for your child to read on their own. These notes are written for you to help your child choose a book and to read it independently.

In school, your child's teacher will often be using reading books which have been banded to support the process of learning to read. Use the book band colour your child is reading in school to help you make a good choice. *Little Spook* is a good choice for children reading at Orange Band in their classroom to read independently.

The aim of independent reading is to read this book with ease, so that your child enjoys the story and relates it to their own experiences.

About the book

Little Spook is scared of something. It isn't the wind, the owl, the bats or the cats. He is scared of the dark. Then a little firefly lights up the darkness and helps Little Spook go out into the dark without feeling scared.

Before reading

Help your child to learn how to make good choices by asking:
"Why did you choose this book? Why do you think you will enjoy it?"
Look at the cover together and ask: "What do you think the story will be about?" Ask your child to think of what they already know about the story context. Then ask your child to read the title aloud. Establish that in this book, the characters are referred to as spooks.
Ask: "What do you know about ghosts? At what time of day do they usually come out in story books?"
Remind your child that they can sound out the letters to make a word if they get stuck.
Decide together whether your child will read the story independently or read it aloud to you.

During reading

Remind your child of what they know and what they can do independently. If reading aloud, support your child if they hesitate or ask for help by telling the word. If reading to themselves, remind your child that they can come and ask for your help if stuck.

After reading

Support comprehension by asking your child to tell you about the story. Use the story order puzzle to encourage your child to retell the story in the right sequence, in their own words. The correct sequence can be found at the bottom of the next page.

Help your child think about the messages in the book that go beyond the story and ask: "Are you scared of anything? What helps you when you feel afraid?"

Give your child a chance to respond to the story: "Did you have a favourite part? Did you think the spooks looked scary? Why/why not?"

Extending learning

Help your child understand the story structure by using the same sentence patterning and adding different elements. "Let's make up a new story about one of the other spooks being scared of something. Which spook is your story about? What are they scared of? How can they feel less scared?"

In the classroom, your child's teacher may be teaching how to read words with contractions. There are many examples in this book that you could look at with your child, for example: *don't, it's, I'm*.

Find these together and point out how the apostrophe indicates a missing letter.

Franklin Watts
First published in Great Britain in 2017
by The Watts Publishing Group

Copyright © The Watts Publishing Group 2017

Series Editors: Jackie Hamley and Melanie Palmer
Series Advisors: Dr Sue Bodman and Glen Franklin
Series Designer: Peter Scoulding

A CIP catalogue record for this book is
available from the British Library.

ISBN 978 1 4451 5431 2 (hbk)
ISBN 978 1 4451 5432 9 (pbk)
ISBN 978 1 4451 6105 1 (library ebook)

Printed in China

Franklin Watts
An imprint of
Hachette Children's Group
Part of The Watts Publishing Group
Carmelite House
50 Victoria Embankment
London EC4Y 0DZ

An Hachette UK Company
www.hachette.co.uk

www.franklinwatts.co.uk

FSC
www.fsc.org
MIX
Paper from
responsible sources
FSC® C104740

Answer to Story order: 4, 5, 1, 3, 2